Harriet gets CARRIED AWAY

Jessie Sima

Simon & Schuster Books for Young Readers

NEW YORK   LONDON   TORONTO   SYDNEY   NEW DELHI

*Harriet* loved costumes.

She didn't save them for Halloween,

or only wear them to dress-up birthday parties.

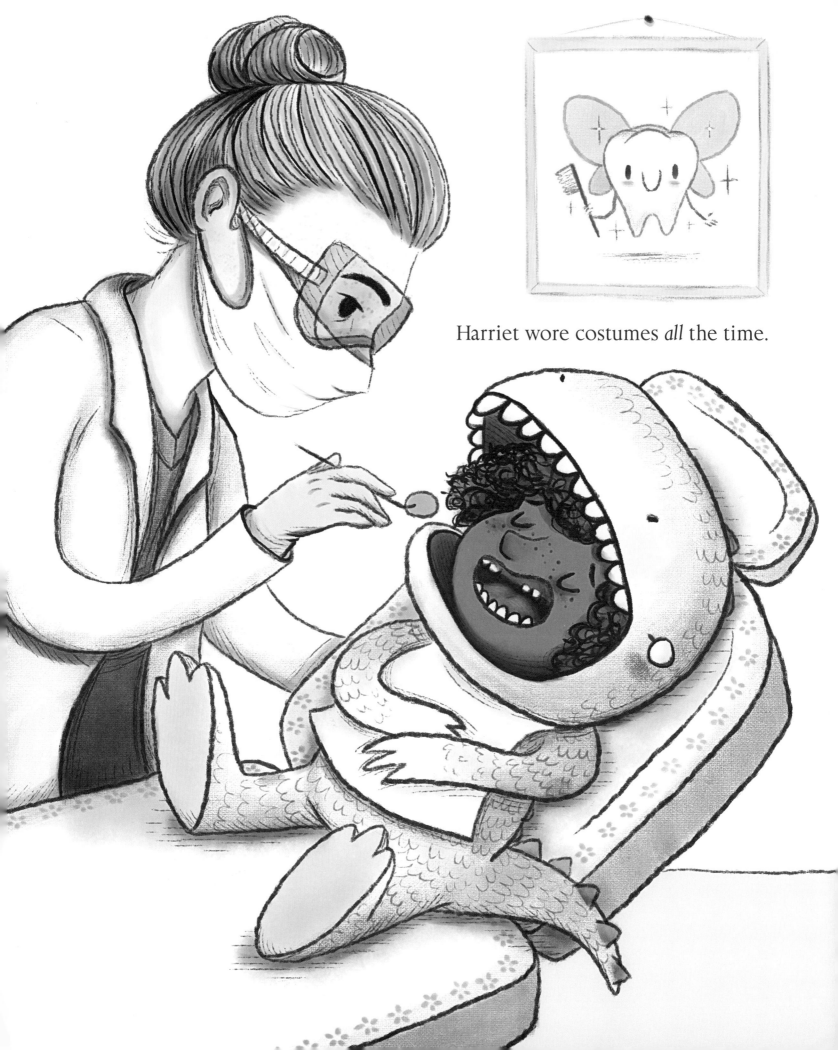

Harriet wore costumes *all* the time.

On the morning of her *own* dress-up
birthday party, Harriet was a busy bee.

"We still need to pick up some snacks
from the grocery store," her dad said.
"And lots of party hats!" Harriet added.

Her dads shared a look. "Okay," they said. "But don't get carried away."
Harriet was sure she could manage that.

She changed into her extra-special
errand-running costume,

straightened her bow tie,

waddled down the street,

through the subway . . .

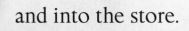and into the store.

Her dads seemed to have
the deli counter covered,

so Harriet set out on a quest for
the perfect party hats.

But instead she found . . .

something else.

Harriet forgot all about the party hats.

She waddled past the check-out lines,

through the city . . .

and out of town.

"Where are we going?" Harriet asked excitedly.

"Back home, of course," a penguin answered. "The city is
a nice place to visit, but I wouldn't want to *live* there."

As the balloons floated farther from the city, Harriet's thoughts floated back to her birthday party.

"Excuse me," said Harriet.
"I don't think I belong here."

"That's okay," the penguins replied.
"Everyone feels like they don't fit in sometimes. Maybe you should lose the bow tie."

But Harriet didn't care about fitting in—
she cared about getting back to the store.

So she straightened her bow tie . . .

and hatched a plan.

And another.

Things were *not* going smoothly.

Harriet was almost out of ideas
when one emerged from the sea.

"Hey!" said the orca. "You're not a penguin!"
"How did you know?!" cried Harriet.
"Penguins don't wear bow ties," he replied.

Harriet realized this orca might just be her ticket home.

So she told him her tale of costumes and penguins and hot-air balloons.

She told him all about her family, and her city,
and the party hats she needed to find.

And when her story was finished, she said,
"I could really use a lift."

"It just so happens I'm heading up north for a family reunion," replied the orca. "I could drop you off along the way . . . in exchange for a fancy red bow tie." This seemed like a fair trade.

As the orca swam, Harriet daydreamed.

Once Harriet could make out the city in the distance, the orca came to a halt. "This is as far as I can go," he said.

So Harriet called in a favor from
some friends she knew from the park.
"We'll take it from here," they said.

Harriet soared back into the store and headed straight for the party hats.

PARTY SUPPLIES

It didn't take long to pick out the perfect ones.

She found her dads at the deli,
just where she'd left them.

"Where did you sneak off to?" they asked.
"I just went to get the party hats," said Harriet.

"Oh, and I could use a new bow tie."

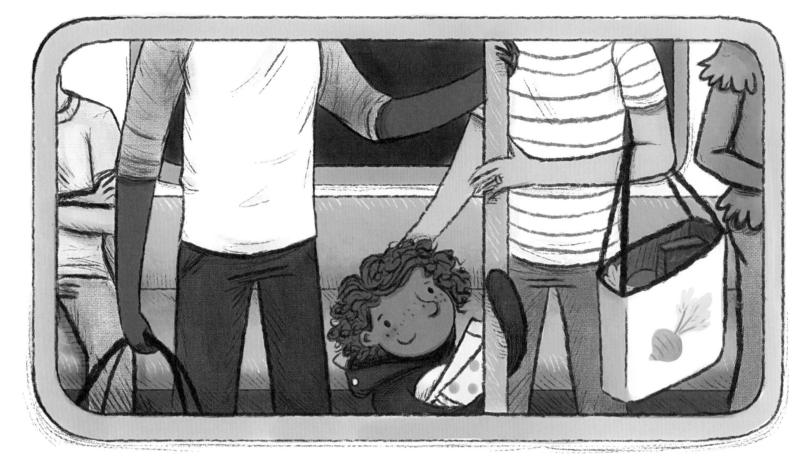

With hats in hand, Harriet waddled back through the subway,

up the street,

and into her room.

She put on her birthday party costume, straightened
her party hat, and headed up to the roof.

The party was a great success and no one got carried away.

Except, maybe, Olivia.

For Rachel,
WHO ALWAYS GETS
CARRIED AWAY WITH ME

SIMON & SCHUSTER BOOKS FOR YOUNG READERS

An imprint of Simon & Schuster Children's Publishing Division

1230 Avenue of the Americas, New York, New York 10020

Copyright © 2018 by Jessie Sima

SIMON & SCHUSTER BOOKS FOR YOUNG READERS is a trademark of Simon & Schuster, Inc.

For information about special discounts for bulk purchases, please contact

Simon & Schuster Special Sales at 1-866-506-1949 or business@simonandschuster.com.

The Simon & Schuster Speakers Bureau can bring authors to your live event.

For more information or to book an event, contact the Simon & Schuster Speakers Bureau

at 1-866-248-3049 or visit our website at www.simonspeakers.com.

Book design by Lizzy Bromley • The text for this book was set in Aries.

The illustrations for this book were rendered in Adobe Photoshop.

Manufactured in China • 1217 SCP • First Edition

2 4 6 8 10 9 7 5 3 1

Library of Congress Cataloging-in-Publication Data

Names: Sima, Jessie, author, illustrator. • Title: Harriet gets carried away / Jessie Sima.

Description: First Edition. | New York : Simon & Schuster Books for Young Readers, [2018] |

Summary: While shopping with her two dads for supplies for her birthday party, Harriet,

who is wearing a penguin costume, is carried away by a waddle of penguins and

must hatch a plan in order to get herself back to the store in the city.

Identifiers: LCCN 2016053689 (print) | ISBN 9781481469128 (eBook) | ISBN 9781481469111 (hardcover)

Subjects: | CYAC: Costume—Fiction. | Penguins—Fiction. | Gay fathers—Fiction. | City and town life—Fiction.

Classification: LCC PZ7.1.S548 (eBook) | LCC PZ7.1.S548 Har 2018 (print) | DDC [E]—dc23

LC record available at https://lccn.loc.gov/2016053689

FIELD
NOTES

Memo Book
Durable Materials / Made in the UK

To Bronwen and David, bear spotters – M. R.

For Sam Williams – D. R.

Bloomsbury Publishing, London, Oxford, New York, New Delhi and Sydney
First published in Great Britain in 2016 by Bloomsbury Publishing Plc
50 Bedford Square, London, WC1B 3DP

Text copyright © Michelle Robinson 2016
Illustrations copyright © David Roberts 2016

The moral right of the author and illustrator has been asserted

A CIP catalogue record of this book is available from the British Library

ISBN 978 1 4088 4555 4

Printed in China by C & C Offset Printing Co Ltd, Shenzhen, Guangdong

1 3 5 7 9 10 8 6 4 2

www.bloomsbury.com

All papers used by Bloomsbury Publishing are natural, recyclable products
made from wood grown in well-managed forests. The manufacturing
processes conform to the environmental regulations of the country of origin.

BLOOMSBURY is a registered trademark
of Bloomsbury Publishing Plc

A Beginner's

Guide to

BEAR

SPOTTING

written by

Michelle
Robinson

illustrated by

David Roberts

BLOOMSBURY

LONDON OXFORD NEW YORK NEW DELHI SYDNEY

Going for a walk in BEAR country?

You'd better make sure you know your bears.

This is a **black** bear.

[FIG. 1. BLACK BEAR, URSUS AMERICANUS.]

This is a **brown** bear.

[FIG. 2. BROWN BEAR, URSUS HORIBILIS.]

And

that is . . .

. . . just plain SILLY.

I don't think you're taking this very seriously.
You ought to, you know.

Bears can be VERY dangerous.

If you get them muddled up, either one of them could **eat** you.

NOW are you paying attention?

Okay, here's what you need to know
before you start walking:

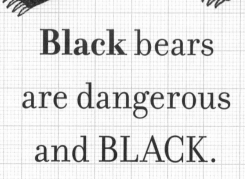

Black bears
are dangerous
and BLACK.

Brown bears
are dangerous
and BROWN.

Although sometimes **brown** bears can be a little BLACK . . .

. . . and **black** bears can be a little BROWN.

Don't worry.
Chances are you won't
even SEE a bear.

Oh, you LUCKY thing!

I think it's a **black** one.

It MUST be.

Brown ones CAN'T climb trees.

Did you know **black** bears weigh around 400lbs?

With a **black** bear, the

best thing to do is back away *s l o w l y.*

This must
be your
LUCKY
DAY.

You've found a **brown** bear too!

With a **brown** bear, the best thing to do is **play dead**.

Although to a **black** bear, that's like an **invitation** to **dinner**.

This would be a good time to use your pepper spray.

Pepper spray works on BOTH kinds of bears.

It makes them
d i z z y.

Or was it hungry?

Yep, DEFINITELY hungry.

Got any porridge?

GUM?!

What on earth are you going to do
with a pack of **gum**?

Of course.
Why didn't I think of that?

Quick!
Run for it!

Oops!

Well, I'm afraid I'm all out of ideas.
Got anything *else* in that bag?

Nope.

Too FLASHY.

That'll
NEVER do.

What did I tell you about
that silly thing?

It's soft and it's silly and it's . . .

...WONDERFUL!

It's working!

Well I never. I take it all back!

Bears *can* be dangerous . . .

. . . but they can also be
    very, *very* sweet.

Psst!

Don't forget the golden rule
of BEARSPOTTING:

Real bears aren't this friendly,
you should only EVER snuggle up to the **stuffed** kind.

Don't say I didn't warn you.